OCEAN
ANIMALS
IN DANGER

SURVIVORS SERIES · FOR CHILDREN

OCEAN
ANIMALS
IN DANGER

by

Gary Turbak

illustrated by

Lawrence Ormsby

Northland Publishing

The artist would like to thank the following biologists and photographers for help in providing research to illustrate the animals in this book: Judith Connor (brown pelican); Bob Cranston (loggerhead sea turtle and right whale); Nora Deans (brown pelican); Jeff Foott (Guadalupe fur seal and sockeye salmon); Elaine Harding-Smith (salt marsh harvest mouse); Masterson (sockeye salmon); Kevin and Cat Sweeney (humpback whales); Tom Ulrich (Steller sea lion); and Norbert Wu (southern sea otter, loggerhead sea turtle, manatee, humpback whales, and right whale).

FIRST EDITION

ISBN 0-87358-574-7
Library of Congress Catalog Card Number 94-13131

Cataloging-in-Publication Data
Turbak, Gary.
Ocean animals in danger / by Gary Turbak ; illustrated by Lawrence Ormsby. — 1st ed.
        p.   cm. — (Survivors series for children)
            ISBN 0-87358-574-7 : $14.95
    1. Marine fauna—Juvenile literature.   2. Endangered species—Juvenile literature.
            [1. Marine animals.   2. Endangered species.]
            I. Ormsby, Lawrence, 1946- ill.   II. Title.   III. Series.
        QL122.2.T87 1994   94-13131
        591.92—dc20

Designed by Carole Thickstun
Edited by Erin Murphy and Kathryn Wilder
Production by Rudy J. Ramos
Production supervised by Lisa Brownfield
Manufactured in Hong Kong by Wing King Tong

Pteranodons died about sixty-five million years ago, when all dinosaurs became extinct. They measured about twenty-five feet (the size of four beds laid end to end) from wingtip to wingtip.

J LoFaro '84

What It Means to Be Endangered

This book is about animals living in the oceans—but not just any animals. The animals in this book are endangered. This means there aren't very many of them. They are in danger of becoming extinct. "Extinct" means the last animal of that kind has died.

Many animals have become extinct. Dinosaurs are extinct. Dodo birds are extinct. Woolly mammoths are extinct. You will never see one of those animals alive. The animals in this book could become extinct, too.

Why Are These Animals Endangered?

Some ocean animals are endangered because their habitat is changing. An animal's habitat is the place where it lives or a special place where it sometimes needs to go. People are building homes and starting farms where the salt marsh harvest mouse likes to live. Humans are using the beaches where loggerhead sea turtles want to lay their eggs. These two animals are endangered because their habitat is disappearing.

Other ocean animals are endangered because people used to kill them on purpose. For a long time, men in ships killed right whales and humpback whales to get meat, oil, bone, and other useful things from their bodies. People also killed Steller sea lions, southern sea otters, and Guadalupe fur seals for their valuable skins. When people kill too many animals, it is called persecution (pronounced *per-si-QUE-shun*).

People also harm some ocean animals by accident. Sockeye salmon can't travel in rivers where humans have built dams. Brown pelicans used to get poisoned by DDT, a kind of pesticide (pronounced *PES-ti-side)* that people sprayed to kill bugs. Manatees sometimes die because they get tangled in ropes or get hit by boats. People don't want to hurt these animals, but sometimes they do so by accident.

What Kinds of Animals Are These?

This book features ten endangered animals that live in or near the ocean. One, the brown pelican, is a bird. Birds are easy to identify because they have feathers. The loggerhead sea turtle is a reptile, a kind of animal that includes snakes and alligators. The sockeye salmon is a fish. The rest of the animals in this book are mammals. Although many of these mammals live in the water, they breathe air just like people. These ten aren't the only endangered ocean animals. There are many others.

Southern Sea Otter

This playful animal lives in the ocean near California. It eats lots of shellfish—animals like clams that live inside shells. Otters float on their backs and put shellfish on their chests. They break the shells by hitting them with rocks, then gobble up the little animals inside.

When a mother otter dives to the ocean floor to get shellfish, she leaves her baby on the surface. The baby floats like a cork until the mother returns. Otters can stay underwater for up to five minutes.

This is a crab, one of the sea animals otters like to eat.

The sea otter's hind feet are webbed, almost like a duck's feet. This helps make it a strong swimmer.

Unlike whales, sea otters do not have blubber to protect them from the cold ocean water. Only their thick fur and their quick movements keep them warm. Oil spills or other pollution can kill otters by damaging their fur and leaving them unprotected.

Sea otters are endangered because people used to kill them for their fur.

Pacific Ocean

United States

Shaded area shows where sea otters used to live before they became endangered.

Flaps of skin cover the ears to keep water out while the otter is under water.

Thick fur helps keep the otter warm in cold water.

Right Whale

A right whale eats by swimming with its mouth open. Water flows into this huge opening. Food in the water—tiny animals like shrimp, called krill— catches on bristles (pronounced *BRIS-sels*) in the mouth. Then the whale spits the other stuff out.

Right whales sometimes stick only their tails out of the water. When the wind hits the tail, it pushes the whale through the ocean like a sailboat.

Right whales are endangered because in the past too many of them were killed. Whalers considered them the right whales to hunt because they were slow and friendly and usually floated when harpooned.

All right whales have these growths that look like warts. They are made of the same material as your fingernails. The largest growth, on the end of the whale's upper jaw, is called the bonnet..

Every year, right whales take two long trips called migrations (pronounced my-GRAY-shuns). Sometimes, they go six months without eating.

Whales breathe through blow holes just as you breathe through your nose and mouth. The right whale has two blow holes.

Beneath the skin, a thick layer of blubber (a kind of fat) keeps whales warm.

Whales have good eyesight, but they depend mostly on their hearing to know what's going on around them.

The whale uses its flippers to help steer through the water.

Sockeye Salmon

This fish lives in the Pacific Ocean, but its life begins and ends high in the mountains. Sockeyes hatch from eggs in Redfish Lake in Idaho. When they are one or two years old, they swim hundreds of miles down big rivers to reach the ocean.

For two years they travel around the Pacific. Then they somehow find the river that brought them to the ocean and start swimming upstream. Only the strongest sockeyes reach

During the breeding season, adult sockeyes turn a bright reddish-orange, and the male's jaw becomes hooked.

No one knows how sockeyes know the way from the ocean to Redfish Lake.

Redfish Lake, where they lay their eggs. Then they die. Even though each female lays about two thousand eggs, fewer than five sockeyes make it back to Redfish Lake in some years.

Sockeye salmon are endangered because they have trouble getting past dams in the rivers.

The female uses her tail to dig in the gravel at the bottom of the lake, where she lays about two thousand eggs.

Salt Marsh Harvest Mouse

The salt marsh harvest mouse does not live in the ocean. Its home is in California at the ocean's edge. Most land animals need fresh water. They would get sick if they had to drink salty ocean water.

The mouse's body is about as long as a stick of gum. It weighs about the same as two pencils.

This mouse is special. It can drink salty water and get along just fine.

The salt marsh harvest mouse does not dig tunnels like other mice. It lives in a grassy nest on top of the ground. On cold mornings, this mouse moves very slowly, but it gets faster when the air gets warmer.

The salt marsh harvest mouse is endangered because people have changed its habitat by building homes where it likes to live.

Thick cover helps protect these mice from predators. This plant is called pickleweed.

This mouse is very buoyant (pronounced BOY-ant), which means it floats easily in the water. It is also a good swimmer.

Steller Sea Lion

The Steller sea lion is as big as a buffalo. It is, however, an excellent swimmer. It can twist and turn and dive just like a fish. In fact, this sea lion catches fish and other small ocean animals for food.

The sea lion spends almost all its time in the ocean. It comes onto land only to breed and have babies. On land, the males—called bulls—sometimes hiss and roar and try to bite each other. They get along better in the water. Steller sea lions live in the Pacific Ocean.

Steller sea lions are endangered because people used to kill them for their fur. Today, they sometimes can't find enough food.

Steller sea lions make long, mysterious migrations. No one knows where they go, but each spring they return to their homes along the coastline.

A long head and neck help the sea lion swim smoothly. Long whiskers help it feel its way under water.

On land, sea lions walk awkwardly on their flippers. In the water, though, they are very graceful.

Manatee

The manatee can survive in the ocean, but it usually lives in bays or rivers. Most American manatees are in Florida, because they like warm water.

Manatees communicate with whistles, chirps, and squeaks.

Although a manatee has tiny ears, its hearing is very good under water.

This animal's nickname is "sea cow." It spends most of its time feeding on plants under water. About every ten minutes it must come to the surface to breathe.

Manatees are shy and gentle animals. If there is a dam nearby, they like to float in the water rushing out of the dam, like surfing.

Manatees are endangered because people used to kill them on purpose. Accidents with boats and at dams still kill some manatees.

Heavy bones help the manatee dive. Manatee babies can swim as soon as they're born.

Some manatees have scars from being hit by boat propellers.

Brown Pelican

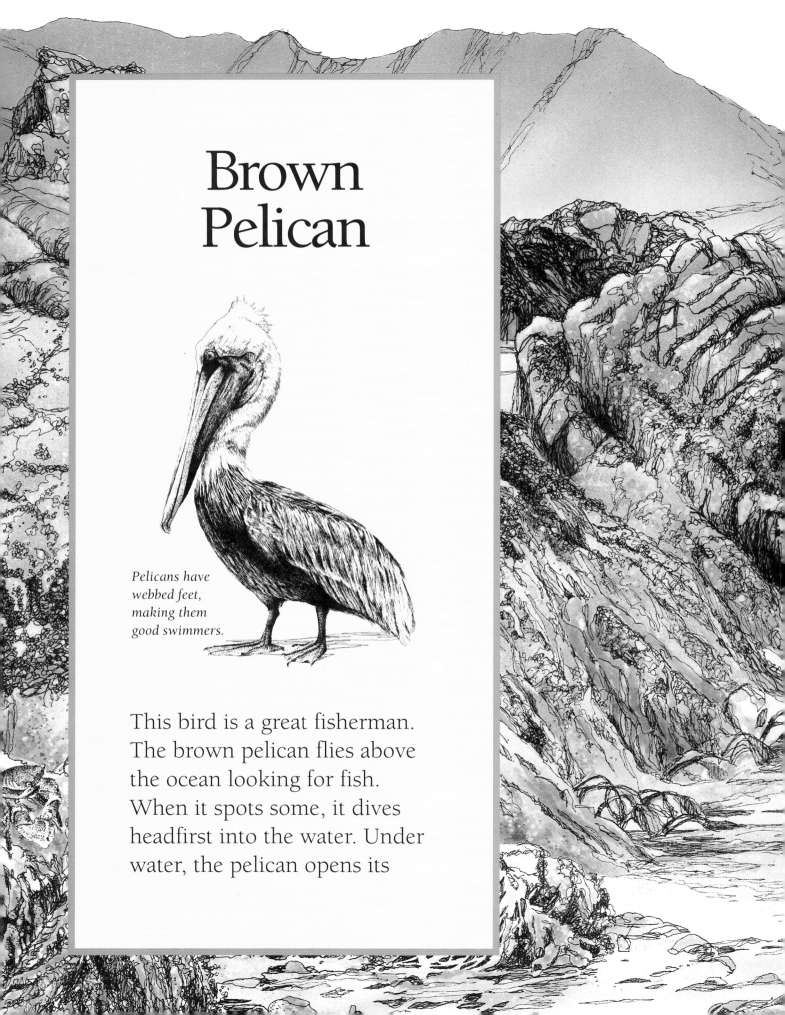

Pelicans have webbed feet, making them good swimmers.

This bird is a great fisherman. The brown pelican flies above the ocean looking for fish. When it spots some, it dives headfirst into the water. Under water, the pelican opens its

huge beak to scoop up water and maybe some fish.

When the pelican returns to the surface, it spits out the water but keeps the fish, swallowing them whole.

Brown pelicans look awkward on land, but they are graceful in the air. They can soar for a long time without flapping their wings.

The brown pelican is endangered due to pesticide poisoning.

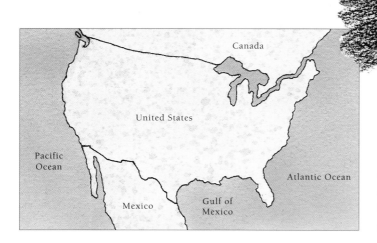

Brown pelicans live in both the Atlantic and Pacific oceans. They usually stay near land, but sometimes they fly twenty miles out to sea.

The pelican's wingspan (the distance from wingtip to wingtip) can be as long as seven feet—bigger than most grown men.

Adult pelicans feed their babies by bringing food up from their stomachs into their big bills. The babies then stick their heads into the bills and eat. It's almost like eating out of a big bowl.

Little pouches under the pelican's skin are filled with air. This makes diving into the water softer for them.

Loggerhead Sea Turtle

This turtle is much larger than the turtles you see around lakes and ponds. One loggerhead turtle can weigh as much as two or three people.

Loggerhead turtles rarely leave the ocean. Each summer, however, some females crawl onto beaches and dig holes in the sand. They lay lots of eggs in the holes, cover them with sand, and then return to the ocean.

Powerful jaws are used to crush shellfish.

This turtle gets its name from its large, wide head.

Strong flippers make this turtle a good swimmer.

Two months later, the baby turtles hatch and squirm their way to the top of the sand. Then they crawl into the water. They grow up in the ocean with no help from their parents.

These turtles are endangered because the beaches where they lay their eggs are often used by humans.

Guadalupe Fur Seal

Most of the Guadalupe fur seals in the world live around Guadalupe Island.

Twice in the past, everyone thought Guadalupe fur seals were extinct. Each time, however, someone discovered a few of the animals still living. Today, almost all the Guadalupe fur seals in the world live around Guadalupe Island, near Mexico. A few also live near California.

These animals stay mostly in the water, but sometimes they come to the shore to rest. When a lot of seals visit land at the same spot, that place is called a rookery (pronounced *ROOK-er-ee*).

Guadalupe fur seals are endangered because people used to kill them for their thick, smooth fur.

Bulls (males) have especially large heads and pointed noses.

Bulls bark, growl, and roar. Females make cow-like sounds.

Humpback Whale

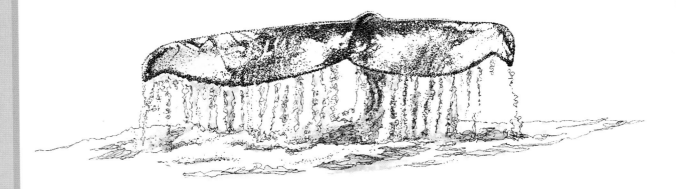

Humpback whales are famous for their singing, but it doesn't sound like human music. Humpback songs are really lots of clicks, groans, whistles, and moans all strung together. Only male humpbacks sing—sometimes all day and all night, hanging head-down in the water. No one knows how or why they do it.

Humpbacks make long migrations that last several months. During migration they don't eat or sleep. Because they are mammals, however, they must come to the surface to breathe air.

Humpbacks also like to breach. This means they jump completely out of the water, then land on their backs with a huge splash. Some scientists think this may knock barnacles (a type of shellfish)

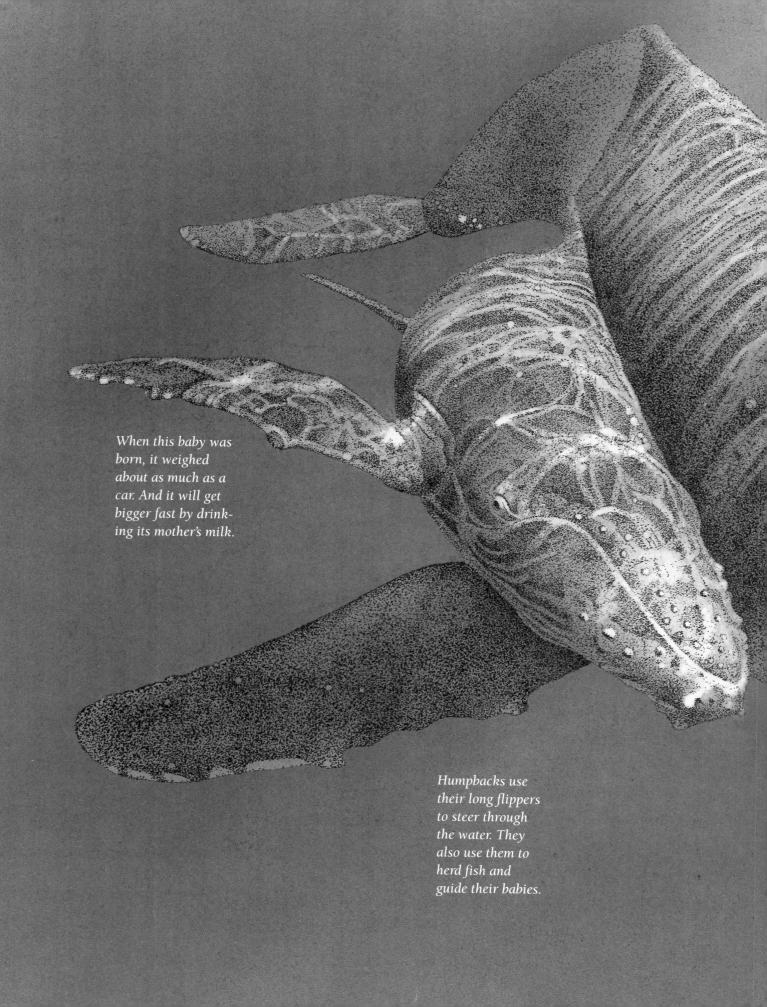

When this baby was born, it weighed about as much as a car. And it will get bigger fast by drinking its mother's milk.

Humpbacks use their long flippers to steer through the water. They also use them to herd fish and guide their babies.

The humpback is a medium-sized whale, but an adult humpback still weighs more than six elephants.

off their skin, but others think they do it just for fun.

Humpback whales are endangered because people hunted them for their blubber, which was made into a kind of fuel oil.

Humpbacks don't have vocal cords like people do. No one knows how they sing, but some of their "songs" last half an hour.

How You Can Help

Do you care about endangered animals? You can help them, you know. One way to help is to learn more about them. You can read more books and magazine articles and watch television programs about these animals.

Once you learn about endangered animals, tell your friends, parents, and teachers. If lots of people know about these animals, they are more likely to be saved and not become extinct.

You also can write letters about endangered animals. The best people to write to are your senators and representative in Washington, D.C. Tell them you want the endangered animals to be protected. Ask your parents for the names of your senators and representative. The address is easy:

Senator _____ (put the person's name here)
U. S. Senate
Washington, D.C. 20515

OR

Representative _____ (put the person's name here)
U. S. House of Representatives
Washington, D.C. 20515

14.95

591.92
TUR   Turbak, Gary
        Ocean Animals in Danger

0-87358-574-7